# The Adventures of Cabeza de Vaca

## Conquistador in Two Worlds

### *(An Imaginative Retelling)*

## Karl Kadie

*Illustrations by Shirley Cosand Smith*

**ISBN: 978-1-7373946-2-4**
**Published by:**
Berkana Publications
Sebastopol CA 95472 USA

**Author's websites and contact information:** Karl.Kadie.blogspot.com

**Cover image and illustrations:** by Shirley Cosand Smith

Printed in the United States of America

**other books written by Karl Kadie:**

    **Poetry:** *Revenge of Nature*
          *The Burning House*

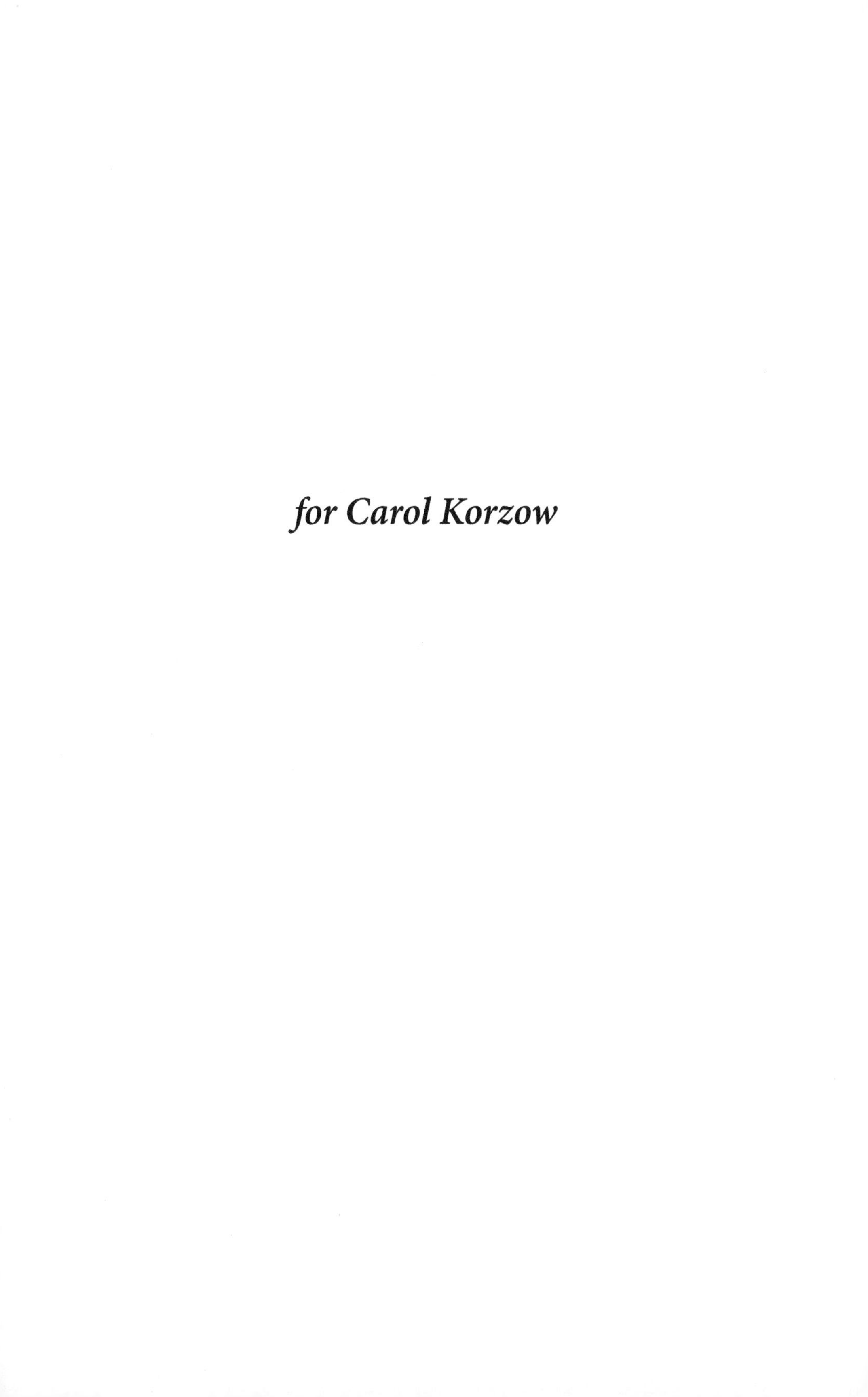

*for Carol Korzow*

# Table of Contents


Preface.................................................................7

1. Stranded............................................................ 11

2. Head of a Cow....................................................... 15

3. To Become a Healer ................................................. 19

4. To Become a Merchant ............................................... 23

5. Broken Trail........................................................ 27

6. *La Relacion* ...................................................... 31

7. The Journey Home ................................................... 35

    A. Carriage Ride to Madrid, 1546........................... 35

    B. History Awakens, 2024 .................................. 36

Notes on Illustrations................................................. 38

Attributions .......................................................... 39

About the Author ...................................................... 41

About the Artist....................................................... 42

# Preface

Alvar Nunez Cabeza de Vaca (1488-1560) was a sixteenth-century *conquistador*. In 1527, this Spanish nobleman and explorer was second in command to Panfilo Narvaez, the governor of Cuba, on an expedition of six ships to conquer Florida. Due to hurricanes and Governor Narvaez's reckless decisions, neither the ships nor the supplies were ever recovered, and nearly all the crew went missing or perished. Cabeza de Vaca was one of the expedition's four known survivors and was lost in North America for nearly a decade. During this time, he traveled on foot from Florida to the Pacific Ocean, living with different Indian tribes. He was a natural polyglot, picking up native languages quickly and easily.

Many years later in Spain, Cabeza de Vaca wrote *La Relacion*, which recounts his adventures in the Americas. It provides a counter-narrative to the *conquistadors'* tales of conquest, and, over time, has proven a reputable resource about native life. The personal history in *La Relacion* is often cited as a testament to human resilience and creative survival.

After a foiled encounter with the Spanish army, he made his way to Mexico City, returning to Spain in 1537. Although he arrived with neither gold nor territory, the success of *La Relacion* salvaged his honor and enabled him to achieve fame and stature with the Spanish court. Cabeza de Vaca secured another post in the Americas, but his plans went awry, resulting in his arrest and return to Spain to face legal charges.

These seven short fictions depict milestones in the life of Cabeza de Vaca, focusing on the select, personal transformations that shaped his American journey:

- *Stranded*—Depicts the outcome of a shipwreck following a hurricane, with most of his crew dead or missing.
- *Head of Cow*—Reveals how his ancestor secured nobility and an unusual title.
- *To Become a Healer*—Describes how he becomes an Indian faith healer as a strategy for survival.
- *To Become a Merchant*—Recounts how he emerges as a merchant between Indian tribes, breaking free of slavery and achieving personal independence.
- *Broken Trail*—Describes his ill-fated encounter with fellow *conquistadors* (after nine years), which results in his arrest and abandonment.
- *La Relacion*—Tells how he pens an account of his travels in America, which achieves acclaim and notoriety throughout Spain.
- *The Journey Home*—Recalls his return to Spain to face trial and clear his name after his arrest as a regional governor in South America.

*The Adventures of Cabeza de Vaca* is based on multiple sources of history. A list of these resources is included in the *Attributions* section. Each fiction is paired with original art that's designed for historical accuracy. Art references are listed in the *Notes on Illustrations* section, as well as in *Attributions*. These fictions and illustrations take full advantage of the archives with the intent of bringing the people, history, and story to life.

# 1. Stranded

*{Governor Narvaez's bad decisions leave Cabeza de Vaca and crew abandoned on the Gulf Coast.}*

After the storm separated us, our raft washed up on the Texas coast. Some dead and some barely alive, shipwrecked without a ship, discards of destiny. Surveying the remnants of our unraveled raft, an image emerged. I saw your face, Governor Narvaez, rising from the ravaged wood, plaguing me with memories of your relentless ambition. I pictured you scratching flint against steel with an arsonist's glee. I wanted to curse into the waters of your whereabouts and proclaim a litany of your sins. But I restrained myself. My men needed to see strength.

It didn't start that way. With the empire and the grace of God filling our sails, we cast off into the Florida Gulf with four ships and four hundred men. You ordered us to abandon our ships to conquer Apalachen, the village of gold. After marching for days, we found nothing but storehouses of Indian maize. We left empty-handed. No gold, and when we returned to the coast, no ships, no supplies, and no food.

Repeatedly, damage outstripped rank until you became the only man I ever despised. Were we merely play toys to serve your glory?

You commanded us to build and launch rafts. With your one eye, red beard, and the expedition's strongest men, your raft was first on the water. In the breeze between us, your honor reeked like spoiled mutton. I planned to confront you when we reached land, but the hurricane drove your craft from my sight.

Though free from your yoke, voices from the dark chamber of my heart called for your raft to never reach shore. Sharks have a nose for the malevolent, and I prayed they'd find your scent easily.

I hate you, Governor Narvaez. It wasn't enough that you caused this mess. You punished us with survival.

# 2. Head of a Cow

*{Cabeza de Vaca is a hereditary title of Spanish nobility awarded in the 12th century, which means "head of cow." It was bestowed on Martin Alhaja, a local shepherd, for marking a hidden mountain pass with a cow skull, which enabled the Spanish army to surprise and win a decisive battle against the Moors. His 16th-century descendant, Alvar Nunez, carried this title into the Americas as a conquistador and explorer.}*

In the *Reconquista*, Alhaja's cow skull marked the turning point in the war against the Moors. Spain rewarded him with wealth, nobility, and title.

Cows mean different things to different people. To Egyptians—mother of the sun and renewal. To Buddhists—calm and holiness. To Hindus—the Ahimsa Principle: bring no harm to the living. But to Alhaja before the big battle, cows were chaos. Each time the Spanish fought the Moors, cattle scattered like storm debris, destroying haciendas and towns. After this battle, order was restored and cows were again cows.

To American Indians, cows were spirits of the earth, generous and reciprocal, while *Conquistadors* were wild and dangerous animals who captured and killed natives, stole supplies and gold.

Cabeza de Vaca did not attack Indian tribes; he joined them. He learned Indian tongues, ate prickly pears, traded between tribes, and carried as much wood as anyone, all the while torn between his Spanish nobility and life as an Indian refugee. Yet he knew he was blessed, that the cow skull hovered above, a halo protecting him from the worst.

For the Americas, he cooked a new soup, an Ahimsa broth sprinkled with holiness, a nurturing, peaceful meal most Spaniards simply declined to eat.

# 3. To Become a Healer

*{After they're coerced to become healers in Southern Texas, Cabeza de Vaca and his Christian brethren thrive}*

When the Malhado rescue us, we are as weak as scurvied sailors. The Indians care for us, share food and shelter. When we recover, their chief tells me, "You eat our food and sleep in our tents but you're useless." He demands we become healers. "Blow on the wounds. Lay hands on them." I scoff, complain that we are not doctors and it's not medically sound. The chief stomps out, raising his bow and arrow to shoot a squirrel. It drops from the cypress as if struck by God.

After that, the tribe withholds our meals. Each day grows more dire, as if our collective canoe had been cast adrift onto a sea of starvation. As my dark heart cries to return to Spain, my heart of light saves me from freefall. I must consider my crew and our survival. If we practice Indian shamanism, we lose our souls. If we don't perform their ritual, we starve.

I retreat to the edge of camp to weigh our options. Animal cries and the rush of night wind are as loud as armies in battle, so loud I hear nothing from the camp. Before long, though, I smell the aroma of frying meat, compelling me to save myself by eating the dead, God's lower creatures. How did I not see it? The wilderness is as hungry as I am. Striving to endure kept us alive but it hasn't kept us safe. How much do I risk by Indian faith healing?

The next day, I enter the tent of a hot, sweating man who clutches his stomach and spits words like musket bullets. Unable to distinguish fever gibberish from language beyond knowing, I put my hands on his chest and blow, saying. "Bless you, my son." Then I recite the Lord's Prayer, followed by an Ava Maria. I pray for him to live so that Christians do not die. I pray for permission to plant seeds of faith: "Heal this man, so he can become Christian."

The following morning, he strides out and proclaims himself well. He rewards me with an animal blanket, precious shells, and a red cedar bow better than anything I own. Two days later, I wake to a crackling fire roasting a rabbit. Men in deerskin loincloths and women with moss skirts curve around my tent, like hands in prayer.

Is this land of want also a land of becoming? Has God let me live so I can imagine more?

# 4. To Become a Merchant

*{Cabeza de Vaca achieves independence as a merchant trading between Indian villages}*

Fed up with poor food and worse treatment, my Spanish friends desert me in this coastal Indian village. If I were not ill, I would join them—no, lead them. But here I lie, uncovered and unprotected, shivering in the sad chill of dark dirt.

The Indians grow bitter because I'm incapable of strenuous work and no longer serve them as a medicine man. Each morning, they force me, now a slave, from warm blankets to wet reeds, where I dig cane roots as long as there's light. At night, my fingers shrivel into red, raw sticks. In the morning, my body is as weak and foul as the stew scooped onto my breakfast seashell. This life won't lead back to Spain, but it does feed my desire for death. I wait for a sign that the Lord is ready to let me go.

The chief complains they have no flint and animal skins, infuriated because his tribe dares not trade with the inland Indians, their enemies, who hold these items in abundance. Their feud makes the trail between villages impassable.

I rise from the reeds to shout, "I can get you flint arrowheads."

The chief spits into the dirt. "Why should I believe you, foreigner?"

I wade onshore and raise my conch shell like a sword. "Inlanders want shells and they'll give me flint for them," I say.

Could trading surpluses between tribes help me to leave this muddy hell? Enable me to walk from village to village to freedom? Two days later, I load conch shells, sea snails, and red ochre onto a wooden sled and drag them many leagues to the interior village. When I arrive, the Indians block my way, suspicious of my intentions. Seeing an opportunity to cultivate suspense, I slowly lift the woven blanket, waiting until the last minute to reveal my bounty, like a priest unveiling the altar. Their brown eyes turn dark with wonder, as wide as mine at first communion.

My outcast status yields an expected benefit: neutrality, truly a gift during negotiations. Two hours later, they serve me venison and maize to celebrate their wondrous new cargo.

Now that I'm a merchant, every tribe hails me with food and feast, fire and tent, often as the guest of honor. I thank the Lord I'm strong, at liberty to travel, and no longer dig cane roots. And if they ask for a medicine man, I'm ready to heal.

# 5. Broken Trail

*{Cabeza de Vaca and Indian friends encounter a small army of Spaniards. For the first time since his arrival in North America, he meets country-men who aren't refugees. He and the Indians honor them with gifts. When the Spanish brigade moves to enslave the Indians, Cabeza de Vaca resists.}*

Enduring won't keep you alive for long. For nine years, I yearned to return to Spain. For nine years, I kept a kernel of culture in memory's soul jar. For nine years, I reinvented myself for Indian hosts, wowing them with European science and Christian faith, anything to safeguard my crew, anything for more time to seek the breadcrumbs of my brethren. I was always on watch for torn, Spanish uniforms, broken lances, and still-warm fire pits.

One day, our trail led to Diego de Alcaraz, commander of a small Spanish brigade. My heart leapt. At last, I'd found my people. Soon, they'd transport me home and I could reunite with loved ones. I'd savor mutton stew and sleep in a bed, protected by a building. But my eagerness got the best of me. What impression did I hope to make with my naked body painted with red dirt, and my black, unkempt hair storming the sky? No surprise that Alcaraz dismissed me.

The Indians gave Alcaraz gifts and offered food. Instead of expressing gratitude, he proposed a nightmare. He bullied me to support his plan to enslave the Indians. How could I betray the people who saved me from starvation, revived me from lost dreams of home, and mentored me in the ways of the new world? "This is madness," I pleaded. "These people have done you no harm."

Alcaraz stepped past me with a flourish. "Pay no attention to the man without clothes. We are returning gods. Serve and you will be safe. Obey and you will be blessed." Red-haired Governor Narvaez had reincarnated as Alcaraz, the Conquista-Monster.

The Indian leader scoffed, "We came from the sunrise, you from the sunset. We healed the sick, you killed them. We came naked and barefoot, you came clothed, horsed, lanced, and gunned. We shared with you; you gave us nothing."

I pulled the Indians aside. "You're in danger. You must leave. I will stay with the Spaniards. They won't hurt me."

"You're mistaken. These are not your people. You're nothing like them. And they dare not attack. We are hundreds, they are forty. Come with us. It's not safe to leave you." I begged the Indians until they gave up. Did they think my reasoning had flown with the morning songbirds? Did they believe the healer/trader with light skin had dived into a vat of peyote stew and refused to climb out?

After the Indians left, Alcaraz's anger bloomed with the dead, black petals of empire. He arrested me as a traitor, marching me into a forest. He deserted me without light or provisions, a virtual sentence of death. I wandered for days without water or food. Each step stabbed me with the loss of my country. Noises at night recalled my wife and family screaming, voices I feared I'd never hear again. When I finally met another tribe, I offered them precious shells and hides in return for drink, meals, and time to grieve. I had saved the Indians from Alcaraz but my Spanish heart was broken. Again.

Yet every nightmare holds room to dream. When I slept that night, I saw myself pick black petals out of a glass of *Tempranillo*, and then drink the wine with unmistakable joy. When I awoke, I sensed Alcaraz was not the only countryman close by. I'd met one *conquistador* on the trail. How long before I'd meet another?

# 6. *La Relacion*

*{After the debacle with Alcaraz, Cabeza de Vaca makes his way to Mexico City, where he arranges travel to Spain. Upon returning to Spain in 1537, he is fifty-seven years old. He arrives with no gold, no new territory, no ships, and only four of the original crew of 400. He feared the crown would see his journey as an abject failure.}*

The crown expected gold and silver. The green, emerald arrowheads Cabeza de Vaca intended to offer had been discarded on the trail during his arrest. What could he do now to salvage his honor, preserve his title, and secure a new appointment? He knew the crown required an account of the expedition, and that he was tasked to provide it. Most ship records were dry, factual reports intended to gloss over the use of supplies and funds. Every *conquistador* knew what the emperor really wanted to hear: we came, we conquered, we succeeded, and here's the gold to prove it.

Not only did he pen *La Relacion* to save his honor and preserve his nobility, but he yearned for the crown to entrust him with another expedition. His core message: Send me again and I'll bring you agriculture, grazing, and mining. *La Relacion*, which recounted his ten years in North America, ricocheted through the Spanish court. His dramatic escapades as a merchant and healer made the New World come alive. His account became others' tickets to dream.

*La Relacion* convinced Emperor Charles to blame Narvaez for the failed expedition (unable to object from the grave). Cabeza de Vaca watched the exotic flower planted in the court garden grow into a jungle, filled with fairies who lured young elites to embark for the wild Americas and inspired soldiers to leave cattle grazing behind.

They signed up without honors or land grants, pleasing the emperor immensely.

After three years, Cabeza de Vaca, now an old man, was appointed to a new post in South America. He sailed west carrying dreams few would share, at least for several hundred years.

# 7. The Journey Home

*{In 1540, Emperor Charles of Spain appoints Cabeza de Vaca as governor of Rio de la Plata, encompassing the southern portion of present-day South America. He arrives in 1541 and is appalled by the treatment of Indians. His reforms abolish slavery and concubines, end mandatory tributes from the Indians, and stop unwarranted entry into Indian homes. These changes are wildly unpopular with local, Spanish nobles, who overthrow his government in 1544, arresting him for mistreatment of the Indians and usurping the emperor's authority. Cabeza is imprisoned for nearly a year, then shipped back to Spain for another trial. In 1546, he's tried, convicted, and banished from the Americas; he's sent to Algeria to serve his sentence. He appeals the decision in 1551, and the decision is reversed. His title and honor are restored and he returns to Spain, where he serves his final days as a regional judge.}*

## A. Carriage Ride to Madrid, 1546

Traveling from one incarceration to the next, Cabeza de Vaca stares through the carriage window, happy to see his home country but sad to feel chains cutting his wrists, arms, and ankles. Despite pain and prison, his heart and mind are unperturbed. Having smuggled evidence of innocence across the Americas, the Atlantic, the Azores, and Europe, he plots his courtroom strategy, confident he'll be absolved.

The nobles of Rio de la Plata, incensed with his reforms as governor, waited until Cabeza de Vaca fell ill, then arrested him. He was tried and convicted before he could mount a defense. This was not the first time nobles preyed on dissidents. They exploited his belief in the ruling class, knowing he'd be reluctant to accuse them of taking slaves and land, of gorging on maize and meat, and of demanding sex from natives unable to resist.

La Relacion may have saved him from obscurity, but not from local lords. As the vast haciendas of Spain glide by, he imagines his fingers tilling the rich, endless American soil. As Spanish field workers scramble to harvest grain, he dreams of the millions of untapped workers an ocean away. He envisions a mountain of American wealth, poised and waiting. Why so difficult to stop subjugating and start trading? He savors the fresh, carriage breeze, knowing the court air will stay foul until his name is cleared.

It would have been easy to slip on conquista gloves and demand tribute, easy to favor fellows over natives. But slavery looks different when you've been a slave. The curve of the boot on your back is never a smile. As Cabeza de Vaca looked in the mirror, he was stunned to see his Indian self staring back. He imagined his nine years as an Indian had come back to berate him, saying, "Remember when you laid hands on folks to cure them? When you sold shells, roots, and arrowheads? When tribes rewarded you as healer and trader? The Indians have done so much for you. However generous the Indians were with their Spanish lords, the native's sole reward has been permission to live. Think, Cabeza! You never hurt or stole from the Indians. Why start now?"

When the carriage rocks, the spires of a Madrid cathedral come into view. Justice is close.

## B.  History Awakens, 2024

Other *conquistadors* made it look simple. Cortes conquered the Aztecs and claimed Mexico. Pizzaro conquered the Incas and claimed Peru, sweetening the pot with shiploads of silver.

Cabeza may not have returned with riches, but he knew better than his compatriots that forging a new world was not as simple as assembling a fort, a church, and silver pieces of eight.*

Few were surprised when history's groundcover—six centuries of research, anthropology, politics, and religion—caught fire with the new, deeper reading of *La Relacion*. When the smoke cleared, Cabeza de Vaca flew boldly from the dying embers, uncompromised by cruelty. Though no one escapes their worldview, Cabeza de Vaca soared dangerously close to the truth.

*16th century Spanish currency.*

# Notes on Illustrations

Illustrations for this project were completed with watercolor pencils, chosen for their flexibility and ability to render precise detail.

The artist aimed for historical accuracy, drawing from museums and educational institutions as primary sources. In this way, she illustrated 16th-century conquistadors, including Alvar Nunez Cabeza de Vaca, showing their physical appearance, clothes, military equipment, bearing, and living arrangements in Spain (e.g., Cabeza de Vaca writing at a desk in Spain). Her drawings of 16th-century North American Indians were based on tribes in the southwest United States, including the Karankawa tribe of Texas, displaying their physical appearance, clothing, tattoos, and hair, as well as their habitat and villages. She asserts that historically authentic illustrations make the work more accessible and relatable.

Detailed references to the Spanish, Indians, settlements, and cultural accouterments are listed under *Attributions*.

# Attributions

## Primary Fiction Sources:

- *Alvar Nunez Cabeza de Vaca, Adventures in the Unknown Interior of America*, edited by Cyclone Covey (translation with commentary of *La Relacion*, by Alvar Nunez Cabeza de Vaca)
- *A Field Guide to Getting Lost*, by Rebecca Solnit
- *Cabeza de Vaca*, by Paul Galante

## Secondary Fiction Sources:

- *Cabeza de Vaca's Adventures in South America*, by Thayer Watkins
- *Cabeza de Vaca Invents the Road Novel*, by Ed Simon
- *Cabeza de Vaca: How Did He Survive?*, from The DBQ Project

## Illustration Sources:

- Raft—Texas Maritime Museum
- Shark—image from freepik.com
- Cow Skull—Texas Maritime Museum, USG, section 107
- Personal Endornments of Indians—Tattoos of Karankawa Indians drawn from descriptions of neighboring tribes; note that no information was available on Karankawa tatoos, according to historian Tom Seiter.
- Clothing of Indians—Adapted from images of 16th century native Americans available on stock photo services.
- Indian Village Scenes—adapted from painting by Frank Weir.
- Images of Cabeza de Vaca—adapted from public domain images shown on US History Scene website.
- Cabeza de Vaca Armor and Spanish Dress—drawn from historic images shown online in stock historic illustrations.
- Guidelines for Use of Art—national regulations for "Creative Commons" used for commercial and non-commercial purposes.

**Special Thanks:**

To Neal Grace for editing the manuscript, Les Bernstein and Amrita Skye Blaine for their critique groups, and Robin Gabbert and Dana Rodney for their reviews and support.

## ABOUT THE AUTHOR

**Karl Kadie** is a poet and author of two collections, *Revenge of Nature* and *The Burning House*. His poetry focuses on history, nature, and relationships, all through the lens of life-changing experiences. His work has been published in *Poetry Catalog, Train River, The Santa Clara Review, Haiku Headlines, Poetry X Hunger, The Sailors Review, Poetry Ink Anthology, New Verse News*, and multiple Redwood Writers anthologies. Mr. Kadie's poems were selected by *Poets for Human Rights* for National Poetry Month in 2023 and 2024, and were featured on the *Calistoga Poetry Walk*. Karl Kadie lives and writes in Santa Rosa, California.

## ABOUT THE ARTIST

**Shirley Cosand Smith** is recognized as a painter, illustrator, and animator, and her work is shown across the country. She is known for her imaginative, whimsical, and humorous creations, often inspired by poetry. Her illustrations have appeared in *Outdoors Unlimited, Communiversity*, and in two books for the San Francisco Maritime Academy. Her animations won first place at the Palo Alto Film Festival and honorable mention at the Ann Arbor Film Festival. She created computer graphics for *Spotted Pony; Mind Scape, Outdoors Unlimited, The Wing Nut*, and *Purple Moon*. Shirley Cosand Smith lives with her cats and creations in San Francisco, California.

www.ingramcontent.com/pod-product-compliance
Lightning Source LLC
Chambersburg PA
CBHW050441200726
48295CB00024B/938